T0131933

JAHAN AKUA

by sara madden

illustrated by hayley helsten

AuthorHouse™
1663 Liberty Drive
Bloomington, IN 47403
www.authorhouse.com
Phone: 833-262-8899

This book is printed on acid-free paper.

ISBN: 978-1-6655-4092-6 (sc)
ISBN: 978-1-6655-4093-3 (e)

Library of Congress Control Number: 2021920807

Print information available on the last page.

Published by AuthorHouse 11/04/2021

authorHOUSE®

"Only from the heart
can you touch the sky"
– Rumi

In the smallest hut and on the shortest hill of the village, there lived a very tall boy named Jahan Akua.

He was the tallest student in his class at school. His knees were level with his teacher's chin.

Jahan Akua wished he were smaller so he would be noticed by the other kids at school.

He had one friend at school named Hadya. Sometimes Hadya only remembered that Jahan was in class when she ran into his legs.

"When are you going to stop growing, Jahan Akua?" Hadya always asked.

His teacher, Miss Magoro, could never look Jahan Akua in the eyes. Jahan Akua was too tall. He was too far up for his teacher to see him.

"When are you going to stop growing, Jahan Akua?" Miss Magoro asked, looking up through her glasses.

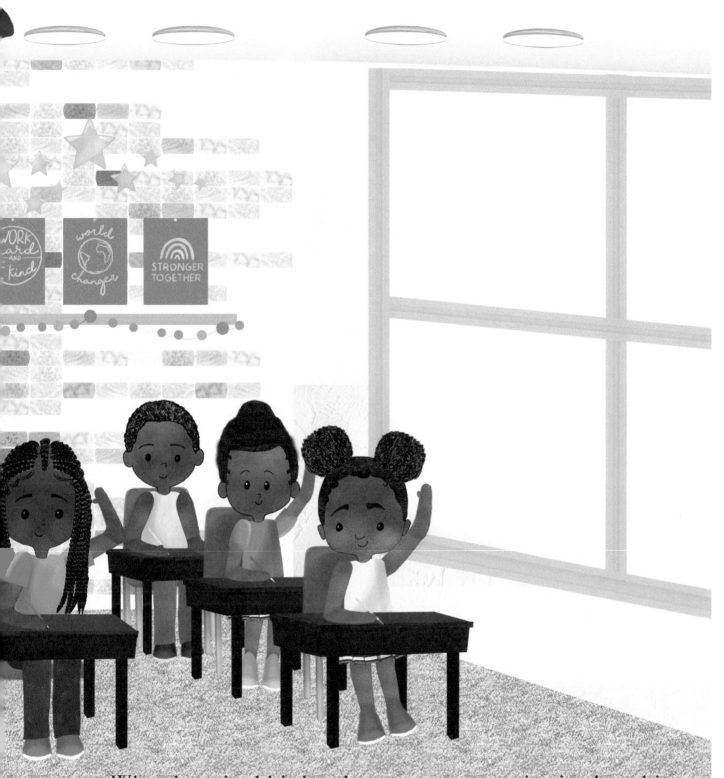

When he raised his hand to answer a question in class, his arm would shoot through the roof of the school. Jahan Akua wished that he would stop growing. He wanted to feel included in his class. He wanted to be noticed.

On his way home from school, he walked through the animal
sanctuary to feed his favorite animal, the giraffe.

The sanctuary worker finally noticed Jahan Akua after
he patted him on his head.

"When are you going to stop growing, Jahan Akua?
I nearly missed giving you your bag of giraffe food, again."

Jahan Akua became sad and ran home.
He didn't like being asked when he was going to stop growing.

As he bent down to crawl into his home, he paused and yelled,
"Stop growing!"

Jahan Akua curled his knees up against his chest
and sat against the wall.

He asked himself like the others did that day,
"When are you going to stop growing, Jahan Akua?"
and then cried into his very large hands.

His mother watched him from the doorway of their home. Jahan Akua looked down and saw her. She was extremely short and round.

She climbed onto Jahan Akua's bent knees so they were facing each other.

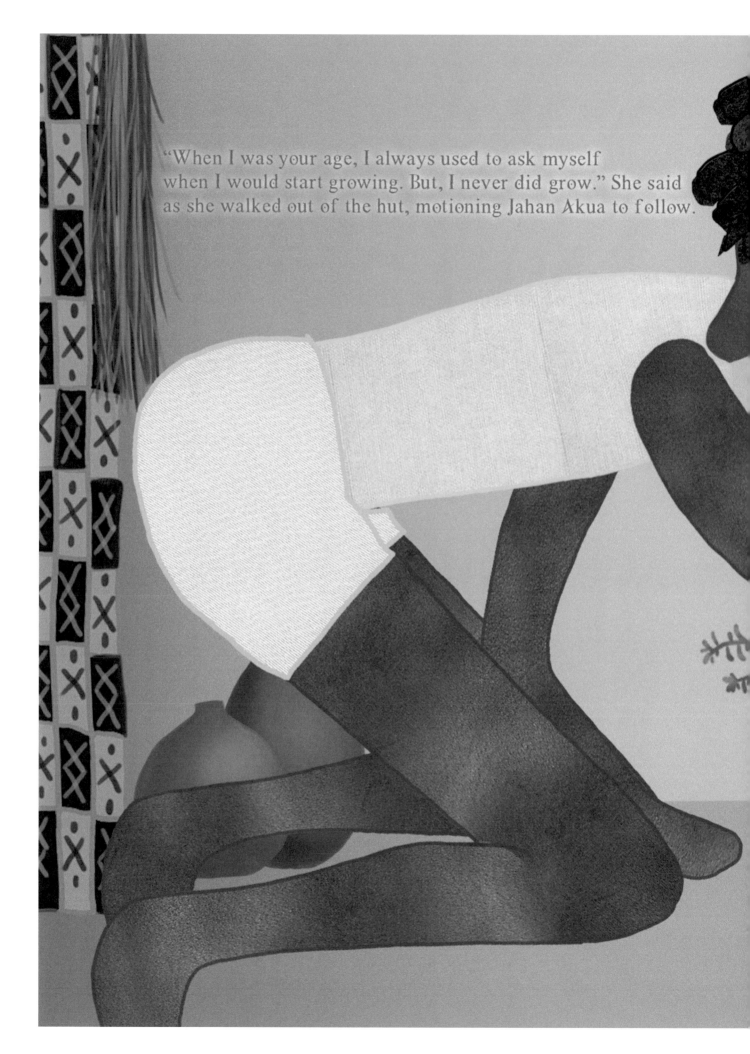

"When I was your age, I always used to ask myself when I would start growing. But, I never did grow." She said as she walked out of the hut, motioning Jahan Akua to follow.

He wiped his tears and followed his mother outside. "I can't make myself stop growing, can I?" he asked.

She shook her head and reached up to take Jahan Akua's hand and said, "You might continue to grow on the outside and can't stop that from happening, but never stop growing on the inside. That's where size matters the most." She placed her hand over her heart.

Jahan Akua smiled as he pictured his heart growing so large he could touch the sky.

The next day at school, Jahan Akua came to school prepared to participate in class. He brought a bell and placed it on his desk. He wanted to be noticed in class and to participate in his lessons from now on.

When Miss Magara asked the class a question, Jahan Akua rang his little bell. For the first time, Miss Magara called on him. With confidence, Jahan Akua answered the question.

"Well done, Jahan Akua," his teacher responded.
"It's about time you made yourself known to the class,"
Miss Magara looked up toward Jahan Akua and they met eye to eye
as Jahan Akua leaned down to meet his teacher's gaze.
"I knew you had it in you all this time."

"Dankie, Miss Magara," Jahan Akua replied.
Hadya smiled up at him from her seat.

From that day on, Jahan Akua used his bell in class. He had found confidence from within himself. His classmates and Miss Magara knew he was there, and liked him just the way he was: large on the outside but especially large on the inside.

About the Author

Sara Madden, who may or may not be a witch, grew up on California's Central Coast. She was raised on donuts and cookies provided by her grandparents' Tan Top Bakery. Her first story was written at age six, titled "I Love My Family," and she's been writing ever since.

Growing up dyslexic (and her continued fun with it into adulthood), Sara always has and always will find comfort in words, imagination, and believing in the unbelievable.

She currently lives in Utah with her adorable family, who may or not be completely bonkers. She has four unreliable guard dogs, eight clocks that refuse to tell time, and four unremarkable typewriters. Buttery popcorn and cinnamon cake donuts are her favorite food. And she never, ever, never, ever, never leaves home without a stick of vanilla or cake batter lip balm in her pocket (her tastes are undeniably fantastic!). In her spare time, she loves to paint and roller skate, but never at the same time-messes are dangerously unavoidable (she knows-she's tried it!).

Look for more of Sara Madden's books coming soon.
Follow Sara Madden and Tallulah Froom online:

SaraMaddenBooks.com
TallulahFroom.com

About the Illustrator

Hayley grew up painfully shy but full of wonder. Her cheesy, adorable parents and seven crazy siblings brought her love and laughter, but she rarely spoke outside her home until she was a teenager. She did, however, find plentyof opportunities to express herself, dancing everywhere she went and drawing on every surface she could find. She fought every day to be happier, healthier, and weirder.

Hayley has grown (slightly) taller and wiser since those days, but she still believes life's greatest joys are dancing in public, laughing until you cry, and eating chocolate chip cookies for dinner.

She now gets to enjoy life with her best friend and husband, Jeffrey. She also loves to play and read with her two adorable children, Lucy Mia and Eric Bradley.They live part time in their small Oregon home, and part time in their VW bus named Magnolia. Both homes are full of kisses and covered in illustrations of all kinds!

Check out more of Hayley's work at HayleyHelsten.com!

Printed in the United States
by Baker & Taylor Publisher Services